LADY LOVELY LOCKS

AND THE PIXIETAILS ™

Silkypup's Butterfly Adventure

By Jean Lewis
Illustrated by Pat Paris

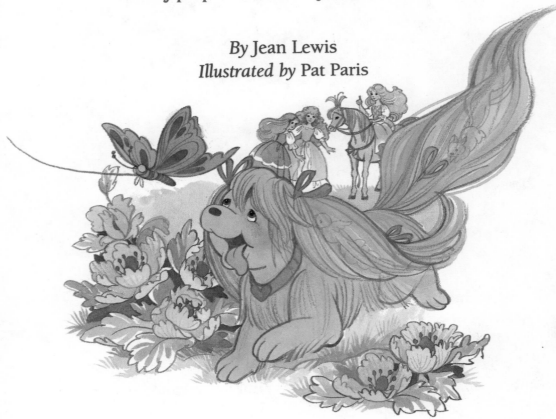

A GOLDEN BOOK • NEW YORK

Western Publishing Company, Inc., Racine, Wisconsin 53404

It was the morning of the Harmony Fair, the annual celebration of the peace and beauty that reigned in the land of LovelyLocks. Everyone was busy getting ready.

Lady LovelyLocks, the beautiful ruler of the kingdom, was wearing her most elegant gown. She tossed her rainbow-streaked hair to summon a special Pixietail.

"Pixieshine," she said, "we await your finishing touch." And Pixieshine, with a wave of her tail, added magical twinkling lights to the hair of Lady LovelyLocks and her dear friends Maiden FairHair and Maiden CurlyCrown.

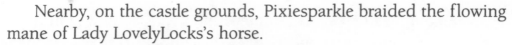

Nearby, on the castle grounds, Pixiesparkle braided the flowing mane of Lady LovelyLocks's horse.

"Hold still, Silkymane," she said. "There!"

Silkypup, Lady LovelyLocks's dog, was delighted with the tiny bows Pixiecolor had tied in her curly coat. She barked with pleasu.

No one noticed a Comb Gnome named Tanglet lurking in the background. Tanglet was out spying for Duchess RavenWaves, the evil ruler of Tangleland. She listened to the Pixietails chatter about the party while they brushed and curled each blade of grass.

"RavenWaves should know about this," Tanglet thought. And off she went.

RavenWaves listened intently to Tanglet's report. She narrowed her eyes and stroked her chin. "This could be my chance," she thought out loud. "If I can somehow get rid of Lady LovelyLocks, I can take over the kingdom, and then I'll be the most beautiful one in the entire land! I'll just invite myself to that party and wait for my opportunity!" She laughed with fiendish glee.

The celebration had already started when RavenWaves arrived
disguised as an old crone. She joined a circle of people watching
Silkypup chase and fetch toys for her mistress. Responding to the
warm applause, Silkypup went around the circle, receiving pats and
praise. But when she got to RavenWaves, she whimpered and quickly
passed by the duchess's outstretched hand.

"Why, that insolent pup!" RavenWaves muttered to herself.

Silkypup jumped into Lady LovelyLocks's arms and licked her face. RavenWaves watched jealously while Lady LovelyLocks hugged her pet.

But then RavenWaves had an idea. "I'll use Silkypup to get to LovelyLocks, since those two are so devoted to each other. But how? Hmm." She broke away from the crowd to think.

RavenWaves passed by Maiden FairHair and Maiden CurlyCrown. They were talking about the next morning's ride.

"Lady is going to want to take a ride to the forest tomorrow," said Maiden CurlyCrown. "She says a long ride refreshes her the day after a big event."

"The same is true for me," said Maiden FairHair. "But not our friends the Pixietails. They'll probably sleep till noon!" The two maidens laughed.

"That's it!" RavenWaves thought to herself. "Tomorrow's the day I capture Lady LovelyLocks! And I know just how to do it!" She hurried off to share her plot with her evil assistant, HairBall.

The next morning dawned clear and bright. It was a perfect day for a ride. Lady reined in Silkymane at the edge of the Forest of Never Known. The forest, which divided the kingdoms of LovelyLocks and Tangleland, was dark and hard to travel in, so the girls stopped at its border.

A huge tricolor butterfly fluttered out of the forest and landed at Silkypup's feet. She sniffed at it, and it darted just out of her reach. Then she followed it.

"Sorry to interrupt your fun, Silkypup," said Lady LovelyLocks, "but it's time to start back."

Silkypup, however, had other ideas. The girls watched as she disappeared after the butterfly into the forest.

Lady LovelyLocks called and whistled, but Silkypup didn't come back. "I'll have to go in and get her," she told Maiden FairHair and Maiden CurlyCrown. "You two can start back. I won't be long." And she plunged into the forest in search of her pet.

Suddenly Lady LovelyLocks heard Silkypup yelping. She broke through the undergrowth and into a clearing. There was Silkypup. The little dog jumped up and down but didn't come to her. She couldn't. She was tied to a tree.

Lady LovelyLocks felt sure it was the work of Duchess RavenWaves, and as she briefly struggled to untie the knots she was even more certain. "These are RavenWaves's super-knots. I'll never undo them myself!" she thought.

"Don't worry, Silkypup, I'll get us both out of here," she told her pet gently. "I know just which Pixietails we need!" She stood up and tossed her hair to summon them.

In Pixietail Park several sleepy Pixietails tumbled off their cozy PixiePetals in the tree house.

"It's Lady!" cried Pixiebeauty. "She's in danger!"

"Hurry!" urged Pixiesparkle. "We haven't a minute to lose!"

Huddled beside Lady LovelyLocks, Silkypup began to shiver. Lady LovelyLocks looked up to find RavenWaves standing over her. Behind her, HairBall dragged a large cage on wheels. He was draped with ropes for tying up the prisoners.

RavenWaves laughed with pleasure. "Now I've got you right where I want you. *I'll* be the ruler of LovelyLocks and the most beautiful of all!"

"We'll just see about that," said Lady calmly. From the rustling overhead, she knew the Pixietails had arrived. She nodded to Pixiebeauty.

Quick as a wink Pixiebeauty twisted vines into an enchanted circle of protection. She leaned down and dropped the circle around Lady LovelyLocks and Silkypup.

RavenWaves was startled by the sudden appearance of the vines, but she decided to ignore them. "Tie these two up immediately, HairBall!" she ordered and opened the cage door.

"I—can't—get—to—them," HairBall grunted.

"What nonsense are you uttering?" RavenWaves said, pushing him aside. But try as she might she couldn't penetrate the circle either. She became flustered and cried out in anger.

"Do be quiet!" said Lady LovelyLocks. "Silkypup's been frightened enough for one day!" Then she called out, "All right, Pixiecolor, it's your turn!" Pixiecolor transformed a forked twig into sharp clippers. She cut Silkypup's rope in an instant, and the dog jumped into Lady LovelyLocks's arms.

"Pixiesparkle," called Lady LovelyLocks, "why don't you show HairBall some of your magic?"

Pixiesparkle beamed her magical light on HairBall. In seconds he was following it around like someone in a trance.

"Stop that!" RavenWaves screamed at HairBall. But he followed Pixiesparkle's dancing light right into the open cage. Then he slammed the door shut!

RavenWaves was nearly choking with rage. She reached through the bars, trying to get HairBall's rope. "I'll try to get into that circle with the rope and lasso Lady LovelyLocks," she thought. "I can't let her get away!"

While RavenWaves struggled to get the rope Lady LovelyLocks signaled to Pixiebeauty, who braided a vine ladder and lowered it.

"Hang on, Silkypup," whispered Lady, holding her close. And up they went into the branches.

RavenWaves had the rope at last. She turned back only to find that Lady LovelyLocks had indeed escaped. She spotted the ladder.

"Well, she won't get far!" she cried and ran to the ladder. As soon as RavenWaves had climbed the first rung, Pixiecolor cut the ladder loose, and it and RavenWaves fell to the ground in a tangled heap.

Working quickly, the Pixietails wove bridges of vines from tree to tree for Lady LovelyLocks to cross. Behind them, they could hear RavenWaves screaming at HairBall and yelling for the Comb Gnomes to come and untangle her.

At the edge of the forest Lady LovelyLocks climbed down from the trees with the help of another vine ladder. She and her friends returned to the Kingdom of LovelyLocks, where Silkymane was waiting to carry them home.

"Yes, this is certainly what I call a refreshing morning," she told Maiden FairHair and Maiden CurlyCrown when she explained their adventure. "It is refreshing to be back in the land of LovelyLocks, where beauty and goodness are everywhere. Especially now that Silkypup is with me again." A happy Silkypup licked her face in agreement.